FAIRY MERMAIDS, THE MULLET RUN

# Dedication

To Charlotte, Sydney, and Annabelle. It takes courage to follow a dream & passion to achieve it. We can't think of a better way to live. We love you.

Mom and Dad

My name is Coral, and I'm a fairy mermaid. Unlike other fairy mermaids who can zoom through the air, I don't know how to fly yet and spend a lot of time at the reef.

Fairy mermaids can change the shape and color of our tails and wings to blend into our environment!

You might think a reef is just a bunch of colorful rocks, but it's actually made of living creatures called coral (that's where I get my name!).

Today Sandy, my best friend, and I are on a mission to hunt for sea glass to make necklaces.

"Are you ready to go to the beach?" I ask.

Sandy swims out of the reef and says "I sure am! I hope we find a blue piece of sea glass this time."

Sea glass is broken glass that has been tumbled smooth by the waves for many years, sometimes hundreds - it's like frosted treasure!

As we swim away from the reef, we bump into Finn, a wise green sea turtle with a shell the color of seaweed.

Did you know some sea turtles, like Finn, can live to be 100 years old! That's a whole lot of wisdom he has collected over the years.

"Hey there, Coral and Sandy! Where are you two going today?" booms Finn.

"We are hunting for sea glass!" chirps Sandy.

"Well, keep an eye out," Finn warns. "It's Mullet run season, reaching the beach might be tricky!"

"Mullet run, that sounds interesting?" I say as my tail flickers nervously.

As we swim closer, the water churns with splashing and flashing scales. Fish are leaping in a frenzy!

Feeling panic bubbling up, I spot Bert, a friendly pelican floating on the edge of the school of fish.

"Hey Bert!" I squeak, "What's going on?"

"Those are Mullet, migrating south," Bert explains. "The Mullet move towards warmer waters every year."

"The splashing is from the Tarpon, who hunt the Mullet. Tarpon can grow up to eight feet long, weigh several hundred pounds and have a big appetite!" says Bert.

"We can't swim through that!" I cry.

Bert chuckles, "Actually, little fairy mermaid, you can fly over it. But it takes courage."

My wings droop, "I'm scared of heights, " I mumble.

"You can do it, Coral!" Sandy encourages me. "Just believe in yourself!"

Bert nods, "Everyone feels scared sometimes, but with courage, you can achieve anything!"

Taking a deep breath, I picture the beautiful blue sea glass. I squeeze my eyes shut, whisper "courage", and with a powerful shake of my wings, leap!

I open my eyes to find myself flying!

The wind whooshes past my ears, and the rush of the Mullet run is amazing from above.

"You did it!" Sandy cheers.

Soaring with newfound courage, I land on the beach with Sandy. After some time, we finally find it – a bright blue piece of sea glass for our necklace.

The perfect ending to a day filled with adventure, friendship, and a little bit of flying courage.

The ocean needs heroes like you! Learn how YOU can make a difference below. Plus, dive into more captivating tales of fairy mermaids with your next book adventure!

www.FairyMermaids.com

Flip back through the story, can you spot the differences between each Fairy Mermaid?

Made in United States
Orlando, FL
01 September 2024

51023841R00015